THE ADVENTURES
OF
CAPTAIN PUMP

THE WORLD'S FIRST
FITNESS SUPERHERO!

THE ADVENTURES

OF

CAPTAIN PUMP

THE WORLD'S FIRST
FITNESS SUPERHERO!

By

Jasson Finney

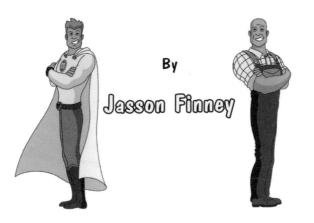

The Adventures of Captain Pump: The World's First Fitness Superhero!
Copyright © 2018 by Jasson Finney
All Rights Reserved

No part of this book may be used or reproduced in any manner whatsoever
without the prior written permission of both the publisher and the
copyright owner.

Book design and layout by Mark E. Cull

LCCN: 2018046034

ISBN (tradepaper): 978-1-939096-05-0
ISBN (ebook): 978-1-939096-07-4

The National Endowment for the Arts, the Los Angeles County Arts
Commission, the Ahmanson Foundation, the Dwight Stuart Youth Fund,
the Max Factor Family Foundation, the Pasadena Tournament of Roses
Foundation, the Pasadena Arts & Culture Commission and the City of
Pasadena Cultural Affairs Division, the City of Los Angeles Department of
Cultural Affairs, the Audrey & Sydney Irmas Charitable Foundation, the
Meta & George Rosenberg Foundation, the Kinder Morgan Foundation,
the Allergan Foundation, and the Riordan Foundation partially support
Red Hen Press.

First Edition
XENO Books is an imprint of Red Hen Press, Pasadena, CA
www.redhen.org/xeno

Contents

Captain's Corner

THE ADVENTURES
OF
CAPTAIN PUMP

THE WORLD'S FIRST
FITNESS SUPERHERO!

CHAPTER ONE

The Origins of a Hero

Do you want to hear the story of the world's first Fitness Superhero? That's right, a real fitness guru whose mission is to help kids all over the universe live healthy and happy lives. This is the story of Captain Pump, a fitness fanatic with pumped-up muscles, who helps kids "Save the Day the Healthy Way."

Unlike most superhero tales, this one doesn't start in a far away land, or some mad scientist's laboratory . . . it starts at an elementary school in a small town where everyone knows everyone . . . maybe one just like yours.

To tell the story of this larger-than-life character, you must first tell the story of a man, a simple man who works at County Public School. A man who is committed to making sure that every student becomes who they are meant to be. A kind and thoughtful man whose dream is to see kids live healthy and balanced lives. He is not a teacher, a counselor, or a principal. He is the janitor, George Basner.

George is an imposing and jovial fellow with a shaved head who sports his trademark overalls, plaid shirt, and work boots. He is very fit and has always lived a healthy life. He learned a long time ago that being healthy means eating well, and being fit means exercising your body and mind. He adopted good eating and lifestyle habits, such as exercising regularly. Even if he didn't feel like doing it that day, he persevered and pushed himself to get the job done. Year after year he kept to his regimen, staying the course to become who he is today. But there is one thing that deeply bothers our friendly custodian. George wants to help the kids learn to adopt the same healthy ways so they also grow up to be fit, healthy, and strong people, but no one at the school seems to take him seriously, or cares that so many of the students are unhealthy. He worries that if they don't turn it around and start treating their bodies well today, their bodies will not be nice to them tomorrow . . . and he is right.

His biggest obstacle is convincing Ms. Barkelott, the principal, that being fit is just as important as getting good grades—they both count, but try getting her to see that. You see, Ms. Barkelott and her staff think George is just a lunkhead with muscles who pushes a broom.

But the one person who sees that George has much more to offer than simply keeping the halls clean is Ashley Johnson, the soft-spoken and kind English teacher who is fit as a fiddle and full of spunk. Ashley lights up a room with her sparkling eyes and infectious smile. She empathizes with George and also wants to see the kids get fit and make healthy choices.

Together, they have the right intentions, but they just don't seem to know what to do to get the students to take a real interest in their own wellbeing. It's not easy for George.

"It's discouraging to see these kids going down an unhealthy path. But what can I do?" mutters the concerned custodian. "After all, I'm only a janitor."

Ashley, on the other hand, knows that there is more to George than meets the eye, and soon the whole world will know it too.

CHAPTER TWO

The Fall That Tells It All

The school bell rings, and the students shuffle by the teacher's lounge where George is on a ladder, changing a fluorescent light bulb. The morning news report plays on the television in the background.

George, distracted by the news report, loses his footing, slips, and falls off the ladder. Trying desperately to catch himself, he reaches for the edge of the ladder but it's too late. BANG! echoes through the hall as he crashes to the floor, hitting his head hard on the ceramic tile. As he lies there, out cold, he has an anxiety-ridden dream where junk food, led by grotesque fudgy creatures, wages a vicious attack against healthy snacks, marshaled by heroic vegetables and valiant fruits. Ashley hears the loud thump from the hallway, and goes into the lounge to see what the noise is just as George is starting to come to. George sits on the floor next to the fallen ladder, dazed and confused.

"George, are you alright?"

"Oh, my head," moans George. "Ashley, it was terrible! There were fruits . . . and there were vegetables . . . and cakes . . . so many sugary cakes! It was a confectionery catastrophe, a vegetable disaster! These giant brownies and these scary-looking cupcakes and those salty chips . . . and they were attacking the watermelons and then the grapes got all in a bushel, and there were seeds everywhere!"

"It's okay, George. Maybe I should take you to see Nurse Placebo," says Ashley.

"Oh no, I'm fine. I'll just get some water and sit here a minute," says George.

As George walks over to the water fountain, he overhears Ms. Barkelott, a husky woman with an attitude to match, sporting spectacles and her hair up in a bun. She's bellowing from the corridor, scolding a pair of students in the hall. "Guido! Myron! Get over here! That's it, you two! You've really done it this time!"

George pops his head out into the hallway and spots Ms. Barkelott escorting the two class clowns to her office while Zack, the captain of the basketball team, and his teammates laugh and look on.

"Honest, Ms. Barkelott, I didn't know that Mr. Blunt was wearing a wig," sputters Guido.

"Uh yeah, we didn't know," agrees Myron.

"It's called a toupee, and you'll have plenty of time to think about that in detention this week!" exclaims Ms. Barkelott, dragging the boys down the hall to her office.

As the principal pulls the two pranksters along, Coach Moe Tivation, a heavyset, frumpy man who lives, eats, and breathes sports, salutes Ms. Barkelott as he walks by.

"By the way, Coach, practice is cancelled this week. Mr. Svelte needs to dig up the soccer field for his science class's night crawler experiment," says Ms. Barkelott.

"Huh? What? A worm experiment?"

"All in the name of science," answers the principal.

"But the championships are coming up! How are we supposed to get ready for the big game?" cries the dejected coach while the principal carries on with her two pranksters down the hall.

George stands dumbfounded in the doorway to the teacher's lounge. He shakes his head in disappointment as he watches Guido and Myron disappear around the corner. As he returns to the business of fixing the neon light fixture, he climbs back up the ladder and suddenly hears a startling noise coming from the other side of the teacher's lounge. He stops and looks around, but no one is there. He returns to the business of the light bulb when he hears the same noise again . . . some kind of muffled sound that seems to be coming from the recycling bin on the other side of the room. "What is that?" mutters George. He slowly starts to climb down the ladder. The noise starts to grow louder and louder.

CHAPTER THREE

The Dancing Bin Speaks

George stands over the bin. He spots a most peculiar sight among the load of recyclable paper: a brown manila envelope covered in stamps and postmarks from countries near and far. From Brazil to Egypt, Canada to New Zealand, and many more. "By the looks of things, this envelope has traveled all over the world. How did it get in the teacher's lounge recycling bin?" wonders George.

George grabs the envelope as the muffled sound grows to what is now a human-like voice coming from inside. He picks it up and shakes it as it begins to talk. "Hey, stop that, you knucklehead! You're making me dizzy in here." George drops the envelope on the ground.

Strangely enough, it thuds as it falls to the floor, as if a heavy object is inside. The envelope starts to speak. "Ouch! That one's going to leave a mark! Come on, let me out already."

George picks it up off the floor and begins to tear it open. He hesitates and the voice grows impatient. "What are you doing? Hurry up already! I can't breathe in here."

George, as frightened as he is curious, finally rips it open and the voice suddenly stops. Inside he finds a comic book. The cover reads:

Captain Pump: The World's First Fitness Superhero!

A very impressive image of a caped muscular man appears below the title . . . a superhero with a cool orange head of hair, dressed in a costume resembling the colors of broccoli, spinach, and carrots. He is wearing a squash-colored cape, a green bean–colored belt, and, to complete the outfit, a "CP" logo across his chest.

As George examines the cover, the caped character—a superhero no one has ever seen before, and a fitness one to boot!—seems to be staring right into his eyes. George stands holding the comic book, staring right back at him. "He looks so fit and confident . . . to be honest, he kind of looks like me twenty years ago . . . back when I had all that hair," mutters the janitor.

As George continues to examine the comic book, the fitness dynamo winks at George and starts to peel himself off of the cover . . . inch by inch he comes to life.

This picture of good health, bigger than a mosquito and smaller than a foot-long sandwich, hops off the cover and into the air, swooping and zipping around like nothing George has ever seen.

Startled, George starts to swing at him like a Major League baseball player. "Ah! Shoo, fly, shoo!" George swats at the little speedster as he would a house fly. "Get lost, you little mosquito!" repeats the frightened janitor. But Captain Pump is just too fast, zipping around his head like a fighter jet.

"Are you done yet?" asks the little fitness guru, laughing. George keeps swinging and missing. Out of breath, he finally stops.

"First of all, I'm neither a fly nor a mosquito, so don't ever shoo me again," warns the Captain sternly. "We have a lot of work to do, George."

"What do you mean? Who are you? And how do you know my name?"

"So many questions. I am Captain Pump, the world's first fitness superhero, and I am going to help you help the kids get fit, and get that principal and her staff to understand the importance of exercise and healthy living."

"Good luck with that," says George.

"You wished you could find a way to help the kids . . . well, here I am. Together we are going to help these amazing young people become fit, healthy, and confident so they can be better at everything they do for years to come," announces Captain Pump.

"Wait, this is too weird . . . this can't be happening . . . I'm talking to a mosquito who claims to be a fitness superhero and . . ."

"I'm not a mosquito!!!"

"Well, none of this is real."

"Oh yeah?"

"Yeah!"

"Maybe this will change your mind!"

Captain Pump grabs George by the arm and yanks him into the comic book. George screams and closes his eyes as they crash through its pages like a speeding locomotive until they reach the last page of the book, smash through the back cover, and begin to free fall. Captain Pump, confident and collected, looks over at a frightened George whose eyes are tightly clenched as he screams at the top of his lungs.

CHAPTER FOUR

Welcome to Pumpland

Captain Pump grabs George's arm. George begins to feel weightless, no longer feeling as though he's falling, but rather . . . flying. He opens his eyes to see a magnificent sight as he and a now full-sized six-foot-two Captain Pump fly over the incredible world of PUMPLAND.

"Wow! I'm flying! I'm really flying!" yells George.

"Yeah, with a little help," chuckles Captain Pump.

Pumpland is a beautiful world filled with bright vibrant colors and a lush green forest with gardens sprouting everywhere. This is a place where fruits and vegetables thrive to monumental proportions and people are in great shape. It's a place where the motto is to help each other, live healthy, and become better people every day.

"Welcome to Pumpland, George! A world where fitness, health, and wellness thrive, where being healthy is the way of life and everyone is welcome. It's also my home. Come on, I'll show ya around."

Captain Pump and George float over the majestic land. "Kids are playing . . . outside!" shouts an excited George.

"Yeah! This is the way of life here. Everyone is active. They play Frisbee, kickball, swim, jump rope, shoot hoops, throw balls, ride bikes, go on hikes . . . and so much more."

"Wow this is amazing!" says George, "Do you really live here?"

"You betcha," Captain Pump affirms proudly.

As they fly by the CP Tower, Captain Pump says, "We develop Pumpsters there."

"Pumpsters?" says George.

"Yeah! We teach the important things in life—being fit, healthy, and kind to each other. Someone who is all those things is what we call a Pumpster."

"Wow, that's cool. I want to be a Pumpster!" exclaims George.

"You think this is cool? Wait 'til you see the farm and the gym and all the Pumpland animals in the forest . . . there is so much to see and do here."

"What's that over there?" George points to a giant carrot emerging from the ground with a giant telescope and satellite popping out of the top.

"That's where I live. It's my headquarters. I designed it myself," says the captain proudly.

"You have a CP School here, too. Just like mine."

They land in front of three majestic purple buildings that look like giant eggplants. "What are those?" asks George. Captain Pump smiles.

"I had a dream about eggplants and decided to build this eggplant building. We aren't sure what we're going to use it for yet, but for some reason I felt drawn to build it, so we are.

Construction should be finished in a few days. I can't wait! And to think it all started with a dream." Captain Pump smiles. "Dreams do come true, you know. Everything starts with a dream. You get what I mean, George?"

"I sure do, Captain, I sure do."

"That's how you create a great life, George . . . first you dream it and then you do it! You know, sometimes you just have to go for it, do what you feel is right like exercising and eating well. You just have to do it!"

George nods. Captain Pump reaches into George's back pocket and pulls out the comic book that brought him to life . . . the MAGIC comic book.

"Now George, listen carefully. What I am about to tell you is crucial. The only way you can get back and forth between the real world and my world is through this magic comic book. Never lose it and make sure it doesn't fall into the wrong hands. Got it?"

"You can count on me," says George.

"And one more thing. No one will ever remember being in Pumpland . . . except for you, of course."

"What do you mean?"

"I mean that when they are here they will know who I am . . ."

"How? What are you gonna do, brainwash them?" asks George.

"No, don't be silly . . . well, kinda. See, the magic comic book erases their memory of ever traveling through it, and, of course, the experiences they had while in my majestic land. When they return they will go back to the place in time they were at before the magic comic book swallowed them up."

"So, no memory and no idea of what just happened?"

"Nope. Nothing but a subconscious idea of what could be a better choice."

"A what?"

"A thought . . . a little voice of reason, you know?"

"Not really, but I'll take your word for it." George takes a second to think. "Oh! I get it . . . a MAGIC comic book."

"Yes, George, a magic comic book. Okay, time for you to go back," confirms Captain Pump. In the blink of an eye, he pulls George into the magic panels.

He moves, once again, through the pages like a speeding locomotive, screaming as he crashes through the scrolling pages until he comes flying out of the book. He lands back in the teacher's lounge, crashing to the floor next to the famous ladder he just fell from minutes ago. Did any of that even happen, or was it all just a dream? Ashley kneels at his side as she did a minute ago.

"Are you alright, George?"

"Yeah, I am fine," insists the dazed janitor.

"Maybe we really should get you to the nurse. This is the second time you have fallen in the last few minutes."

George lights up like a Christmas tree.

"Wait. The second time?"

"Yes . . . okay, let's go see Nurse Placebo," insists Ashley.

"No, no, I'm alright, Ashley. I just need a glass of water and I'll be fine."

"You are a strange man, George. Okay. But if you fall one more time . . ."

"Yes. One more time and I will escort myself to the nurse's office. I promise. What is that you are eating, by the way?"

"It's leftover grilled eggplant from my dinner last night. It's my favorite. Do you want some?"

"No thanks. I'm not really hungry right now."

George remembers the giant purple building he just saw in Pumpland.

"Eggplant is your favorite?" repeats George.

"Yes, I love it!"

Ashley leaves the teacher's lounge as George pulls the comic book from his back pocket and flips through its pages as the frames all of a sudden start to move. Like watching a live movie unfold in front of your eyes. "Wow! The frames actually move?" Out of nowhere the Captain himself appears and starts going through the pages with George.

"Yes, George, the frames move in real time. See George, this magic comic book lets you see what's happening with the kids here in the real world. All you have to do is open it up and you'll see what's going on right now in this moment."

"Really?"

"Here . . . look for yourself."

George sees Guido and Myron sitting in detention with Ms. Barkelott, while the next frame shows Mr. Blunt fixing his bad toupee in the mirror, and finally, Mr. Svelte digging up the soccer field while Coach Moe shakes his head in disbelief.

"Okay, so how do we get these kids in shape?" asks George.

"Simple, we'll teach them in my world to make them better here in your world."

"What? What do you mean?" says George.

Little Captain Pump lands on George's shoulder.

"I picked you to be my representative here in the real world, George, because you genuinely care for these kids . . . just like I do."

"Why do you need a representative here anyway?"

"Well, here is the thing George. You are the only one that can see and hear me in your world. To everyone else I am invisible. In fact, I don't even exist."

"So you mean I am the chosen one?"

"You could say that. So what do you say George? Are you in?"

George furrows his brow as he mulls over the Captain's proposal.

"Okay, count me in," says George proudly.

"I knew I picked the right man for the job! It's going to be great, George. I am going to help you get these kids on a path to health and wellness."

George looks at him. "How are we going to do all that?"

"You'll see, but right now I have a date with Tina Turnip. Can't keep her waiting, you know."

With that, Captain Pump disappears into the magic book while George is left standing there a little confused.

"Me, a superhero's representative?"

The powerful voice of the Captain resounds in George's ear.

"Remember, we are a team now . . . and whatever you do, don't lose that book!"

CHAPTER FIVE

The Beginning of a Superhero's Representative

The friendly janitor flips through the Captain Pump comic book as he enters the hallway outside the teacher's lounge. "This is unbelievable. To think me, a real superhero's representative."

His eyes fixed on the page's scrolling frames, George sees Mr. Blunt barreling down the hall in a haste when all of a sudden, "Look out, you big oaf!" then a horrendous BOOM! The muscular custodian collides with Mr. Blunt and then CRASH!!! He sends the math teacher flying into the lockers, knocking his toupee askew.

"Why don't you look where you're going, you giant klutz!" says Mr. Blunt as he stomps off, quickly tugging his toupee back into place. "Sorry, sir," whispers an apologetic George.

As Mr. Blunt rounds the corner, still trying to fix his toupee, George makes his way down the corridor. Broom in hand, he starts to sweep up the hallway littered with candy bar wrappers and empty chip bags.

He steps on a piece of discarded chewing gum, now stuck to the bottom of his boot. He stares down the hall at the parade of junk food trash and shakes his head. "Help these kids get fit and healthy? This is not going to be easy."

"Maybe not, but it is sure going to be fun," echoes Captain Pump from deep inside the pages of the magic comic book.

"I'm going to regret this," George mumbles. Ashley calls from behind.

"Who are you talking to, George?"

"Who, me? No one . . ."

"I'm worried about you, George. You have been acting pretty weird ever since you fell off that ladder and hit your head."

"No need to worry about me. I am fit as a fiddle."

"I have been thinking about what you said earlier, about the kids."

"Oh, that! Don't mind me . . . The kids are fine," says George, reluctantly.

Ashley is shocked at George's sudden indifference.

"Oh, okay? Well, see you later then, George."

"Wait, Ashley, come back!" yells George as she disappears around the corner.

"I am such an idiot!" mutters George.

"I'll say!" pipes up a disappointed Captain Pump. "Why didn't you tell her the truth?"

"You mean that I talk to a foot-tall cartoon character who claims to be a fitness superhero who lives in a giant carrot in some magical land where everyone is fit and healthy?"

"Yes!" affirms Captain Pump.

George storms off. The Captain follows him, hovering over his head.

"There is nothing wrong with having a fitness superhero on your side, and especially nothing wrong with having a beautiful and caring friend here in the real world."

George turns on a dime, grabs the little dynamo out of the air and looks him square in the face. "You leave Ashley out of this."

George lets him go and continues down the hall as the Captain straightens his cape and lands in front of George's face.

"Don't you ever grab me like that again. I may be small but I will take you on anytime. Do you understand?"

"Sorry."

"Okay. Apology accepted. What is wrong with you?"

"I am scared to tell Ashley . . . she'll think that fall did something to my brain if I tell her the truth."

"The truth is always the best way to go, George. Lying only gets you into deeper and more serious trouble . . . every time!"

"I'm not lying. I'm just withholding information, that's all."

Captain Pump narrows his eyes and looks at George. "Spin it any way you want, George. You're still not telling her the truth!"

"I'm not going to tell her. Case closed!"

"Fine. I can't force you to tell her or do anything for that matter. I can only tell you what I think, and then it's up to you to make your own decision."

"Did you come here to help the kids or to bug me?"

"You can't help others until you help yourself, George!"

Captain Pump disappears into the comic book in George's back pocket, leaving George standing there in thought.

"RING RING! RING! The school bell sounds as kids come flying out of their classrooms. A steady chatter fills the halls as they filter past a confused George.

"Basner! Hey, Basner!" yells an irritated Ms. Barkelott. "The toilet is overflowing in the boys' bathroom."

"Be right there, Ms. Barkelott." George shakes his head. "I should have been a gardener."

George is plunging the toilet when Guido and Myron come into the bathroom.

Meanwhile . . . in PUMPLAND . . .

Captain Pump flies over his domain and gets a flashing red alert on his superpowered CP watch. He pulls a quick U-turn over the mountain tops and beelines into his carrot headquarters. As he sits at his control desk, his "real world" monitor shows Guido and Myron in the bathroom as George comes out of the stall holding the plunger. Captain Pump listens in on the conversation through his real world monitor.

"All good, boys?" asks George.

"Yes sir, thank you for asking, Mr. Basner," Guido answers politely. George leaves the bathroom.

Captain continues to watch the real world monitor as Guido and Myron continue to talk.

"That is not fair," says Guido. "She embarrassed us in front of everyone."

"Yeah, she embarrassed us," agrees Myron.

"I have a plan to get back at her after school."

"Yeah! Yeah! A plan," agrees Myron.

As the two plan their revenge, Captain Pump zips out of his window and takes off into the Pumpland sky. His super-powered Pump Fit watch flashes bright red, indicating trouble ahead.

Back in the REAL WORLD . . .

George sits at his desk in his janitorial storage room, or as he likes to call it, his office, having his morning protein shake looking at the newsfeed on his phone. He grabs a big meaty sandwich from his lunch bag and is about to take a bite when Captain Pump appears out of nowhere, hovering over his sandwich, inches from his mouth.

"We have a problem," announces the Captain.

"Where did you come from?"

"The magic comic book in your back pocket . . . like always."

"I know where you came from . . . Geez! Can you please stop popping up everywhere like that?"

"Have a look at this."

Captain Pump pulls out his tablet and plays George a video of Guido and Myron plotting their revenge on Ms. Barkelott. George shakes his head.

"Don't get discouraged, George. This is a good thing."

"A good thing?" asks George. "How is knowing that two of your students are plotting revenge on their principal a good thing?"

"Because, genius! Now that you know what they are doing, you can stop it before anything bad happens."

"Oh yeah! Didn't think about that."

"Speaking about thinking, have you given any thought to letting Ashley know about . . ."

George puts down his sandwich and sighs.

"It's not that I don't want to tell her, but who would believe me? I mean, I'm having a hard time believing it myself."

The captain pats him on the shoulder.

"Give it some time, buddy. But for now, we have a situation to take care of."

George pulls the magic comic book from his back pocket.

CHAPTER SIX

The Plot Thickens

Across the street from CP Elementary is Snack's Corner Store, a hangout where the students have gathered for years. It's a junk food jungle with shelves full of candy, chocolate, and specialty sugar-infested treats that everyone loves. Guido and Myron walk in while the friendly owner, Mr. Snackadou, pops out of the back room.

"Hello, boys," greets Mr. Snackadou. "Great timing! I just got in a new shipment. These are too good to pass up and they are only for my favorite customers. They are one of a kind, you know!"

The store owner shows the boys a tray full of specialty candies, bags of gooey treats, and chocolates.

"Wow! Thanks, Mr. Snack. These look really great!" says Guido. We'll take them all. Pay the man, Myron."

"Yeah, really great," agrees Myron as he hands the sugar supplier the money.

"Nice doing business with you boys," replies Mr. Snack.

The boys smile and head back towards the school. Myron stuffs his face with the newly bought treats.

"Easy, Myron! Don't eat all our profits. We can charge a premium for these babies," confirms Guido.

"Yeah, a premium," agrees Myron with powdered sugar covering his shirt.

Captain Pump and George peer into the magic comic book as they witness the exchange of goods. George is fuming mad!

"I had no idea they were selling this stuff! That explains all those weird wrappers."

"One problem at a time," says the Captain. The attack on Ms. Barkelott is our priority right now. This is what we are going to do . . ."

Captain Pump whispers into George's ear when his CP watch starts to vibrate and flashes a bright red light.

"Oh no."

"What's wrong?" asks a concerned George.

"Gotta go, George!"

With that, Captain Pump disappears into the pages of the magic comic book while George continues to watch Myron and Guido in the school yard ironing out the last details of this afternoon's attack.

"So we're all good?" asks Guido.

"Yeah, yeah we're good," affirms Myron.

"We strike when the bell rings. Got it?" asks Guido.

"Yeah, yeah when the bell rings," agrees Myron.

Meanwhile . . . in PUMPLAND . . .

Captain Pump flies over the CP Tower, an impressive mushroom-like structure that stands in the middle of town where, along with creating Pumpsters, it houses the scientists and researchers of Pumpland.

A red light flashes from the top of the needle on the peak of the tower as the captain glances at his CP watch, still flashing bright red. As he approaches the tower in full flight, its top flips open and the Captain disappears into its mouth.

A state-of-the-art facility equipped with wall-to-wall flat screens, monitors, and giant digital maps of the surrounding areas. Posted on the screen is a "Wanted" wall displaying the bandits that pose a threat to the Captain and his land . . . none more dangerous than the notorious . . . Freddy Fudge.

Freddy Fudge is a huge and menacing creature who looks like a giant gooey chocolate treat. A cross between Bigfoot and a fudge brownie, he hypnotizes his prey with his gruesome eyes and entices them with sweet, fattening treats. His ultimate goal is to get the kids of Pumpland to join his band of junk food addicts.

The Captain gets briefed by his Pumpster patrol.

"What do we have?" asks the concerned, caped fitness guru.

"Captain, this was just posted on PumpTube. It's already gone viral. You need to see this."

One of the security Pumpsters hits play. Freddy Fudge appears on the screen.

"Citizens of Pumpland. It is I, Freddy Fudge, your sweet tooth's favorite friend. Soon you all will be my subjects. I will infest the whole land with my sugary ways. No one is safe . . . and I mean no one. Captain, that includes you. So beware and prepare . . . the sweet invasion is near. I will make junk food reign from there to here. Mwahahaha!"

The captain stands stoically, looking around at his Pumpster patrol. "This must be stopped. I want a full report on my desk in the morning. Freddy Fudge needs to be unsweetened."

Captain looks at his watch, which still flashes red. "Oh no! Guido and Myron." In a flash, the Captain flies out of the tower into the Pumpland sky at lightning speed.

CHAPTER SEVEN

Ready, Aim, Learn!

Back in the REAL WORLD . . .

RING! RING! RING! The bell rings to signal the end of the school day. The kids fly out of their classrooms. George empties a garbage can as Captain Pump flies out of the comic book in his back pocket.

"C'mon, George!" yells the little superhero with great haste. "They're headed to the parking lot!" The Captain grabs George by the collar and pulls him through the back door to the parking area where Guido and Myron hide behind the dumpster next to the parked cars. Ms. Barkelott exits the school and heads toward her vehicle, hands full with bags.

Guido motions to Myron. "Get ready. Here she comes," says Guido. The boys take their position at the corner of the dumpster ready to launch the attack. Myron reaches in his bag and pulls out two cartons of eggs. He hands one to Guido.

"Cool! You got the extra-large ones too," says Guido.

"Yeah, yeah, extra-large," affirms Myron.

Ms. Barkelott stands at her car door, fishing for her keys in full view of Guido and Myron. Each one is armed with a big white projectile. They give each other a final look as they wind up and . . . out of nowhere, George appears.

"Hey! What are you two doing here?"

"Nothing, Mr. Basner. We were just picking up loose garbage and throwing it in the dumpster. Weren't we, Myron?"

Myron looks at Guido, a little confused. "Yeah, yeah, throwing it in the dumpster."

"Really? I suppose you found those eggs among the garbage?" asks George.

"Huh? Oh, yeah!" answers Guido.

"Time for a little trip."

George opens the magic comic book as Captain Pump pops out when . . . SWOOP!!! The book suddenly sucks the unsuspecting duo and George into its pages.

The captain leads the way as the group screams at the top of their lungs, crashing through each page, one by one.

The three fall uncontrollably. Guido and Myron continue
screaming as George covers his eyes. Meanwhile, Captain Pump
punches through the pages like a heavyweight champion until
they reach the end of the book. Then ... BOOM!! Guido, Myron,
and George come flying out the back cover of the magic comic
book and crash-land into the animated world of Pumpland.

In PUMPLAND . . .

The three stand in the CP Tower control room with computer screens lining the walls. "Excuse me, fellas, but what do you think you're doing?" asks a hulking Captain Pump.

"Ah man! It's Captain Pump," says a defeated Guido.

The Captain pulls a tablet from his pocket and starts clicking away, changing the images on the wall-to-wall screens. George stands next to the Captain while Guido and Myron look on.

"We were just going to exercise our throwing arms, weren't we, Myron?"

"Yeah, our throwing arms, yeah!"

"On what and whom were you planning on exercising those throwing arms? Not on Ms. Barkelott and her car . . . were you?"

"No sir, not us," says Guido. "We would never do such a terrible thing."

"Wouldn't you?"

"No, Captain Pump," says Guido. "We would never do such a thing."

"Lies, lies . . . such lies. Let me show you what damage you could have caused and, more seriously, the harm you could have done to Ms. Barkelott. Take a look at this."

The Captain hits a play button. The wall transforms to a movie of Guido and Myron winding up and throwing egg after egg at Ms. Barkelott. Startled, she hurries to get her keys out of her purse. The eggs keep coming as though they are being thrown by an automatic pitching machine. Unable to get to her keys fast enough, she is hit again and again, egg yolk streaming down her face as she breaks down crying. Guido and Myron smirk at each other.

"You think this is funny?"

"No . . . but she embarrassed us in front of the whole school," insists Guido.

"And why did she do that?" asks an impatient Captain Pump.

"Because we pulled on Mr. Blunt's wig?"

"Yes! And embarrassed HIM!" explains the Captain.

"Yeah, I guess we did. So she did to us what we first did to him."

"That's right. It didn't feel so nice, did it?" asks the Captain.

"No sir," admits Guido sadly.

"Yeah, no sir," agrees Myron.

"If you think that's bad, watch this."

Captain Pump hits play on his tablet. The screen plays a different scenario. This time, as Guido and Myron start launching the eggs at Ms. Barkelott, she panics and slips on the egg-covered pavement and falls to the ground, hitting her head against the car door. An ambulance takes her away.

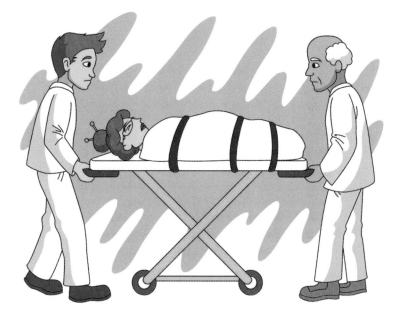

"What happened to her?" asks Guido.

"Well, she hit her head and had to be taken to the hospital."

"Oh no! Honest, Captain Pump . . . we never meant for anything bad to happen," Guido assures him.

"No one ever wants bad things to happen. They just do . . . when you do foolish things and make bad choices! Do you understand?"

"Yes sir, we understand," confirms Guido.

"Yeah, we're sorry," repeats Myron.

"Well, sorry is not always good enough, but lucky for you, you still have a chance to make this situation right. So tell me, boys, how do you think you could make this a happy ending for everyone?"

"What do you mean?" says Guido.

"Well, how could the two of you turn this disastrous situation into a great one?"

"I dunno," says Guido.

"You two think about it. Remember, boys, life is always about choices. It is up to you to make the right ones. I will give you one more hint, one more word of the day that you should always remember and apply in every area of your life: RESPECT! Do you know what that means, boys?"

"I think so . . ." Guido and Myron say in unison.

"It means you always treat people with manners and in an appropriate way," explains the Captain.

"I guess we made a big mistake," says Guido.

"Not yet . . . you still can stop what you might do."

"George!" beckons the Captain, who gestures at the magic comic book in his back pocket. "It's time to take these boys back."

"Okay. Gotcha!"

George opens the magic comic book as Captain Pump pulls him, Guido, and Myron into the scrolling frames. Once again, they fall through the pages as Captain Pump leads the way. BAM! BAM! BAM! One after another, the Captain crashes through page by page, plowing through like a bulldozer. Guido, Myron, and George freefall and scream all the way until . . . BOOM! They come crashing to the ground back in the real world.

CHAPTER EIGHT

The Right Choice

Back in the REAL WORLD . . .

Eggs in hand, Guido and Myron stand at the corner of the dumpster in the parking lot as Ms. Barkelott fishes through her purse for her keys.

Captain Pump and George watch the scenario play out in the magic comic book as the boys wind up.

"This is ridiculous! We can't just stand here and watch this poor woman get pummeled with all those eggs," states an irritated George.

"Hold on, George. Give them a chance."

George stands there and continues watching the scene unfold through the magic comic book. Ms. Barkelott is having trouble finding her keys. The boys give each other a final look, nod, and wind up when suddenly . . . Guido retreats and grabs Myron's arm just as he is about to launch the attack.

Guido looks at a struggling Ms. Barkelott and says to Myron, "Wait! Maybe this isn't such a good idea. I mean, what we did to Mr. Blunt was wrong and we deserved to be punished for it."

"Yeah, yeah, it was wrong," agrees Myron.

"It looks like Ms. Barkelott is having trouble with all those bags. Maybe we should show some RESPECT and go help her?"

"Yeah, yeah, we should go help her."

The boys drop the eggs and head towards Ms. Barkelott who continues to struggle with her keys.

"Can we help you, Ms. Barkelott?" the boys asked in unison.

Surprised, Ms. Barkelott acknowledges the boys. "Well, yes, you can. Thank you, boys. I appreciate it."

"It's our pleasure," says Guido. "Besides, we know what we did was wrong and we just want to tell you that we are sorry."

"Well, thank you. That is very grown-up of you to say. I accept your apology, but the one you should be apologizing to is Mr. Blunt."

"Yeah, yeah, apologize to Mr. Blunt," agrees Myron.

"And there he is right now," Ms. Barkelott points out as she gets into her car.

George looks at Captain Pump in amazement as they continue to watch the scrolling pages. Guido and Myron apologize to Mr. Blunt, shake his hand, and watch him drive away. George, like a proud papa, smiles and gives Captain Pump a high five.

"I told you, George. Never underestimate the power of a fitness superhero. You see, fitness comes in many forms besides the physical. It includes emotional and mental fitness, too."

"I will never doubt you again, my friend. I promise."

"Don't make a promise you can't keep, George."

"What is that supposed to mean?"

"It means exactly what I said. We won't always agree and sometimes we won't always believe in what the other is doing. But as long as we support each other and treat each other with RESPECT, we will be a good team."

"Okay."

"Instead, how about promising me you will tell Ashley about this whole thing?"

"Why are you so insistent that I get Ashley involved?"

"Because you want her to be," says the Captain.

"What about you? How did that date go with Tina Turnip?"

"What does that have to do with anything, George? If you must know, there never was a date and there isn't a Tina Turnip either. I guess I don't want to be alone, just like you."

"Yeah. So we are a lot alike after all."

"We have more in common than just our pretty faces, George," jokes Captain Pump.

"It sure isn't the hair," adds George.

Captain Pump runs his hand through his thick orange 'do.

"Yeah, we sure don't have that in common," laughs the mighty one.

"Thanks," says George.

"For what?" asks Captain Pump.

"For picking me as your superhero representative."

They both smile.

"I am glad I chose you too. I wouldn't have it any other way," says the Captain.

He disappears into the scrolling frames. George closes the magic book, folds it, and puts it in his back pocket.

Minutes later . . .

Back in the school, George returns to emptying the garbage can as Guido and Myron walk over.

"Hey Mr. Basner," says Guido. "Do you know anyone who could use a few dozen eggs?"

"Of course. Did you know that the egg is the perfect protein, and protein is crucial to building muscle and a strong body?"

"Wow! We didn't know how healthy they are. Thanks, Mr. Basner."

"They are great in an omelet, hard-boiled, or just fried by themselves. A great way to start the day the healthy way."

Meanwhile . . . in PUMPLAND . . .

The Captain smiles while he watches the conversation unfold on his real-world monitor. "That George is a fast learner."

CHAPTER NINE

The Pumpland Praise

In PUMPLAND...

Captain Pump, wearing a hard hat, stands in front of the giant eggplant buildings along with a few Pumpland construction workers.

"The buildings will be ready in a few days, Captain," says one of the workers.

"What are you planning on doing with them anyway?"

"Oh, I have big plans for this place. It all came to me in a dream last night. Everyone in Pumpland will thrive here."

"Wow! I can't wait," answers the construction worker.

"Me neither," says the Captain.

Meanwhile . . . back in the REAL WORLD . . .

George finds an envelope with his name on it taped to the door of his office. He opens the envelope and finds a "Get Well" card inside from Ashley. George smiles and puts the card in his shirt pocket as he locks up for the day.

Meanwhile . . . back in PUMPLAND . . .

At his carrot headquarters . . .

Captain Pump sits at his control desk typing on his keyboard and looking at the screen while mumbling to himself, "This will be perfect. It's the right time and I think Pumpland needs it!"

Captain Pump pulls a sheet from his printer and scans the data into his tablet.

"This is exactly it!" he says to himself, looking at the printout.

At that moment, the Captain hears a soothing chirping sound from a distance . . . it begins to get closer and soon, sitting on the Captain's shoulder, is a lovely bluebird, angelic and beautiful, singing to him.

"Ah, hello, Christina, my favorite bluebird. Thank you for your beautiful song. Look what I am doing. I can't wait for all of Pumpland to see."

The bluebird chirps and flutters her wings in approval. The captain smiles and flies into the Pumpland sky.

Meanwhile . . . back in the REAL WORLD . . .

George sits in the bleachers overlooking the football field where Mr. Svelt continues to dig for worms. He pulls out the card that Ashley gave him, smiles fondly, and mutters to himself.

"Maybe that little mosquito is right. Maybe I should tell Ashley about all this . . . nah! She would think I lost it. She sure is amazing."

Meanwhile . . . back in PUMPLAND . . .

In the CP Tower . . .

Captain Pump stands in the CP Tower laboratory with the Pumpland science specialists. He pulls up the data and posts an image on the screen.

"I want you to make me this."

The scientists look at the image in awe and begin enthusiastically drawing plans, discussing options and conferring with Captain Pump about this top-secret project that will soon amaze, thrill and surprise all of Pumpland.

"Spare nothing. Do what you have to do to get this done."

As the Captain and his team start the secret project, there is a disturbing meeting taking place within the Pumpland Mountains . . . where Freddy Fudge and his clan reside.

In Freddy Fudge's den . . .

Deep in the mountains, this towering beast stands in front of his followers: a band of sugary villains loyal to Freddy's cause. They listen carefully as he speaks.

"My sweet scoundrels, the time has come to wage the war on healthy foods and healthy ways."

The crowd cheers.

"We must destroy Captain Pump once and for all!"

The junk food warriors cheer louder as they chant and pledge allegiance to the ferocious one.

"Soon, my friends, everyone will be addicted to us and we will forever have our way with them. The sweet and sugary will prevail!"

The crowd erupts into a Freddy frenzy, cheering and chanting as they celebrate the imminent sugar invasion.

Back at the CP Tower . . .

The scientists are hard at work as Captain Pump looks on.

"This will be the best thing ever," he says.

Captain Pump takes off into the Pumpland sky. He glances at his CP watch, now flashing a bright green light, signaling that everything is well in Pumpland and the real world . . . for now.

THE END

Captain's Corner

Hey kids! Wow! What a whirlwind of events! As you witnessed firsthand, Guido and Myron needed a little lesson in RESPECT and how to make the right choices.

Did you see how happy Ms. Barkelott was to see the boys offer to help her? And the boys felt great after choosing to help instead of hurt. I'm so proud of them for choosing the right thing to do.

Remember, you will always have the luxury of making choices in life, and if you make the right ones, you will always move forward in a positive direction.

Don't worry if you make a wrong choice here and there. Mistakes are something we all make. Remember, there is nothing wrong with being wrong, because we all are at one point or another. It is a part of being human.

The important thing is that you learn from those mistakes— be aware of how your actions affect other people, and also how they affect you. And always be responsible for what you say, and also what you do. That is the key!

If you hurt someone with your words or your actions, apologize . . . say you are sorry . . . AND MEAN IT! Just like Guido and Myron apologized to Mr. Blunt for pulling off his toupee. People will appreciate you taking responsibility for your actions and RESPECT you for doing so.

You and I are a team now. Just like George and I are a team. As your Captain, I will be here to help you get fit and healthy. I am here when you feel there is no one to talk to. I am here when you feel alone and discouraged. Got it, my little Pumpster-in-training? Good!

Don't hesitate, my Pumpster friends. If you feel down or alone, come and see me in Pumpland. Here you will have a whole bunch of friends to learn from. Remember, Pumpland is place where everyone is welcome, and that includes you!

Captain's Gym

Now, an important component to being fit is making sure you exercise and move your body every day! So every time we get together I will leave you with a fitness lesson here in the Captain's Gym.

This is a place that will help you become confident and strong, resilient and durable. Heck! You will be like me if you follow all of the wonderful lessons I have for you. Are you ready to start becoming the fitness guru you were meant to be? Awesome! Let's get started.

Do you have your sneakers and workout clothes on? If you don't, you better go change, 'cause it's time to sweat and pump up those muscles!

Consider me your personal trainer and together we will get you fit and healthy in no time. Now for today's fitness lesson.

Phase One

I want you to be active and move your body just like we do here in Pumpland. It is the only way to a healthy life.

Spend sixty minutes running, jumping, skating or playing a sport. Do this every day to make your body strong, fast, and resilient. This will keep you energized and your heart healthy. Then you can be on your way to becoming a full-fledged Pumpster.

Now before you continue reading, I want you to go complete Phase One. Then come back and we'll continue your Pumpster workout.

Make sure you do it before you continue reading. I will know if you did or not. In Pumpland we always run, jump and play. It's the healthy way!

Did you do it? Did you run, hop, and jump today? Awesome! I knew you could do it. And I bet you feel better too. You have more energy and you feel ALIVE.

You are now ready for Phase Two of your Captain Pump workout. This part is really cool. Are you ready? Here we go.

Phase Two

This is your exercise routine. It is the one I started out with years ago when I was your age. These are easy, fun exercises that you can do alone or with your friends. The important thing is to just do them every day. So here is your everyday workout.

1. Do five push-ups.

Do as many sets of five push-ups as you can. How do you do a push-up, you ask?

It's easy-peasy. All you have to do is push your body up off the floor. Do what I do. Look at the picture and copy me. Are you in the same position as I am? We'll call this the "start" position, okay? Now keep your body straight as a board like me. Then bend your elbows until your chest and knees touch the floor. Then push your body up off the floor until you are back in the "start" position.

If you have trouble, change your "start" position to having your knees on the floor and just use your upper body.

The key is to do them slowly. That will make you stronger and give your muscles a great workout. Now, when you can do that easily and you feel strong, start doing sets of ten pushups.

2. Now I want you do you ten sit ups.

Lie on the floor on your back with your knees bent, like I am. Then put your hands behind your head. Don't pull on your head though. Then raise your shoulders off the ground until you can't anymore. Feel your abdominal muscles contract. This is how you get strong abdominal muscles like mine. When you get good at doing this ten times, go for fifteen, then twenty. Soon you will have a strong core and that is a good thing!

3. Finally, I want you to do ten squats.

Your legs have very big muscles that get tired fast. So make sure you do these the way I am showing you. Let's get in a "start" position. Stand with your knees bent and your upper body reaching to the sky. Bend your knees while keeping your upper body reaching to the sky until you are in a sitting position, and return to your standing one. Do these ten times.

Awesome! You are so on your way to becoming a Pumpster! Now make sure you do both phases every day, and also make sure you feed your body well. Which brings me to the next part of being fit and healthy.

Phase Three

CAPTAIN'S CUPBOARD

The saying, "You are what you eat," is so true. What you put into your body will play a huge factor in how healthy your body will be. So feed it right. I want you to have two different servings of vegetables each day. To build muscle you need protein too. Make sure you get plenty of vitamins and minerals by eating a well-balanced diet full of fresh fruits and vegetables, nuts and seeds, lean meats, grains, and water . . . don't forget to drink plenty of fresh water. I love my fruits and vegetables, and here in Pumpland we grow them all. If you eat a variety of green, yellow, orange, purple, red, and white fruits and vegetables, you will always have a healthy body. I eat my fruits and vegetables like the colors of the rainbow. Not only do they taste great, they make me feel great! And they will make you feel great too.

Captain's Final Words

The last thing I want you talk about is the importance of being RESPECTFUL. I know we talked about it earlier, but it's so important I want to talk about it again.

Be respectful to your parents, your brothers and sisters and your teachers, your coaches, your friends, and most of all, yourself. Help someone when you see they can use it. Say a kind word to someone and mean it. And always encourage people who need it.

Well, I have to go now. Wait till you see the top-secret project we are working on here in Pumpland. I can't wait to show you! So come back and see us. And remember, I am your fitness superhero, and we are partners in this journey of becoming fit and healthy to Save the Day the Healthy Way!

Well, that's it for now.

This is Captain Pump, your fitness superhero, signing off.

Until we meet again, my Pumpster friend.

Captain Pump!

About the Author

Jasson Finney has worked for many years in the fitness and entertainment industries. His performing experience began in his teens as a drummer in several touring rock bands. Today, Jasson is a working actor and stuntman in both film and TV.

After graduating from the University of Ottawa with a degree in the school of Human Kinetics, he dedicated many years to helping people attain their fitness and health goals. A seasoned fitness and lifestyle professional, Jasson has helped hundreds of people regain their health and fitness prowess.

Over the years, Jasson has gained invaluable experience creating, promoting, and delivering professional "winning attitude" team building, fitness, and lifestyle programs. Such examples are his "Business Athlete" and "Hockey Athlete" programs targeting those wishing to live a healthy life, improve performance, and boost confidence by applying athletic concepts to become champions in their own right. *The Adventures of Captain Pump* is the culmination of his experience as a coach, trainer, and motivator that is sure to help kids Save the Day the Healthy Way!

A regular fitness expert for CBS, Jasson is passionate about making a difference in people's lives. His mission is to help, teach, and guide people towards a healthy lifestyle as well as entertain and create in film and TV.

If you had to sum him up in one word it would be "big." He is a big guy, with a big heart who always thinks and does big.